Snow Penguin

Tony Mitton   **Alison Brown**

BLOOMSBURY
LONDON OXFORD NEW YORK NEW DELHI SYDNEY

This little Penguin can never stay still.
He's always in search of excitement and thrill.

In a world full of water, of ice and of snow,
what will he find there? He's eager to know.

Staying close to his home is a bit of a bore . . .
so our brave little Penguin sets off to explore.

He waddles right out to the brink of the ice
where the sea looks inviting, so blue and so nice.

He gazes out seaward and doesn't look back,
so he can't see the ice is beginning to crack.

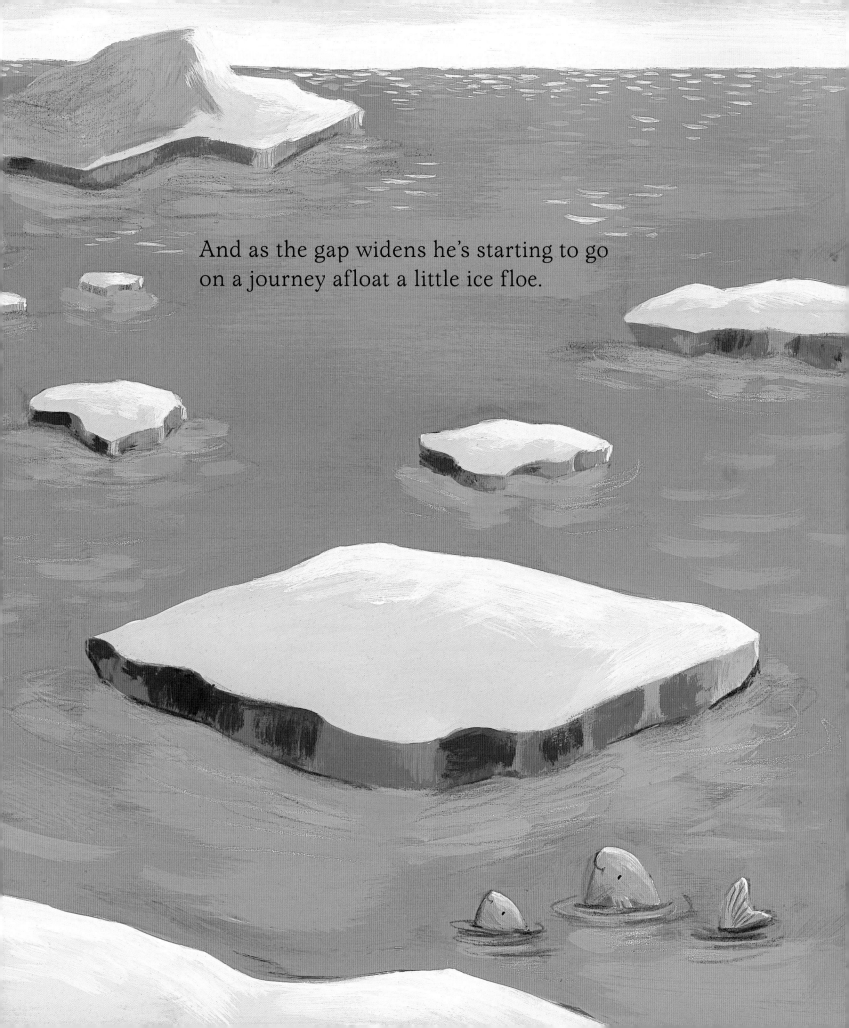

And as the gap widens he's starting to go
on a journey afloat a little ice floe.

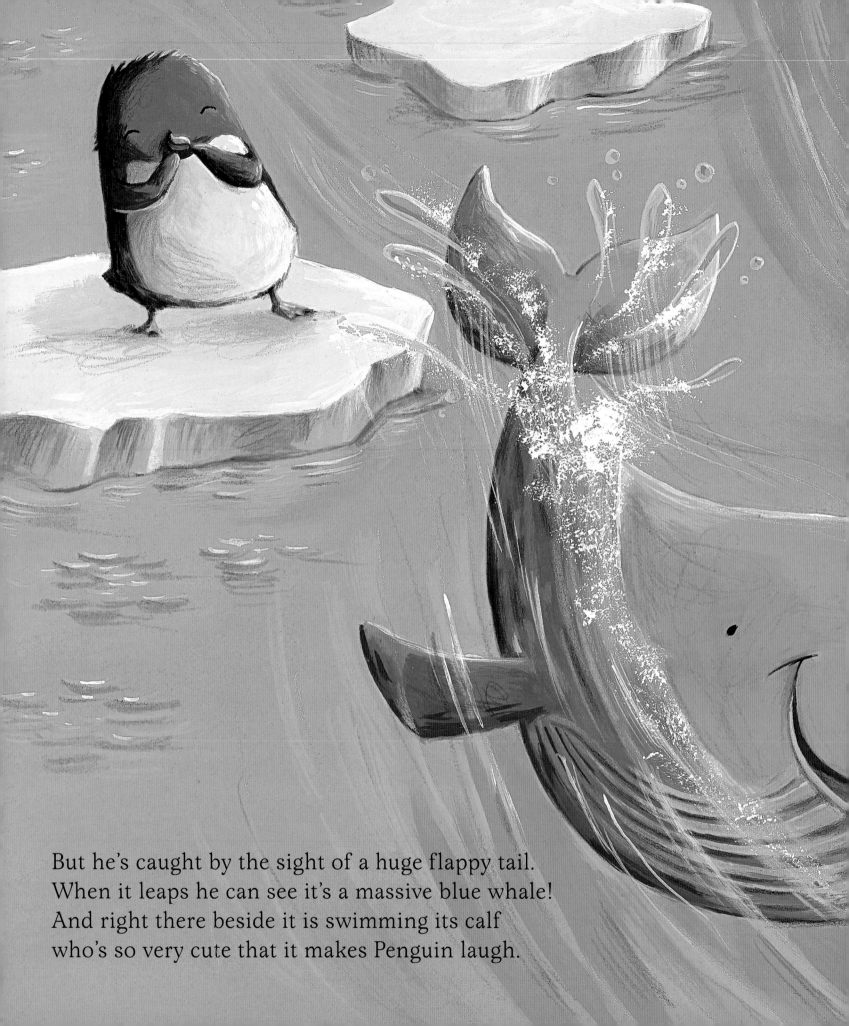

But he's caught by the sight of a huge flappy tail.
When it leaps he can see it's a massive blue whale!
And right there beside it is swimming its calf
who's so very cute that it makes Penguin laugh.

Then a wild school of orca go racing nearby
and he thrills to the sound of their echoey cry.
The little ones learn to be agile and quick
as they call to each other with whistle and click.

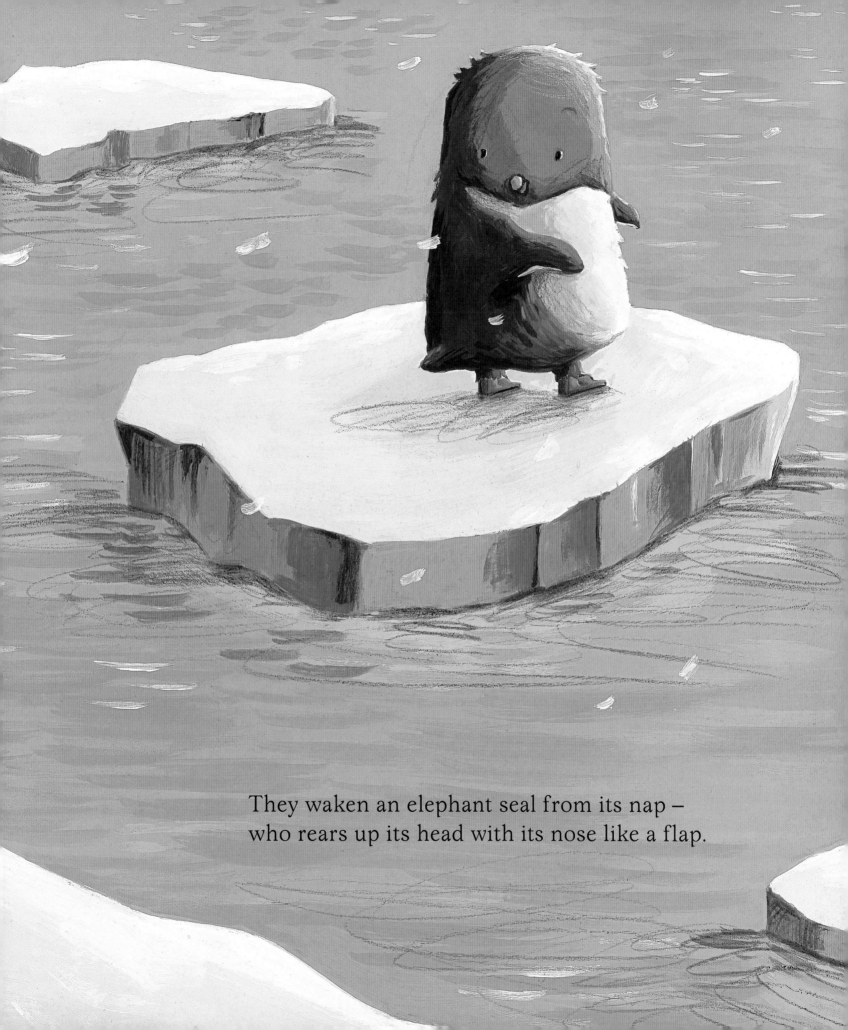

They waken an elephant seal from its nap –
who rears up its head with its nose like a flap.

And here is a sea lion that's called up her cub
to give it a nuzzle, a nudge and a rub.

It makes Penguin feel how a hug would be nice
and he notices then he's alone on the ice . . .

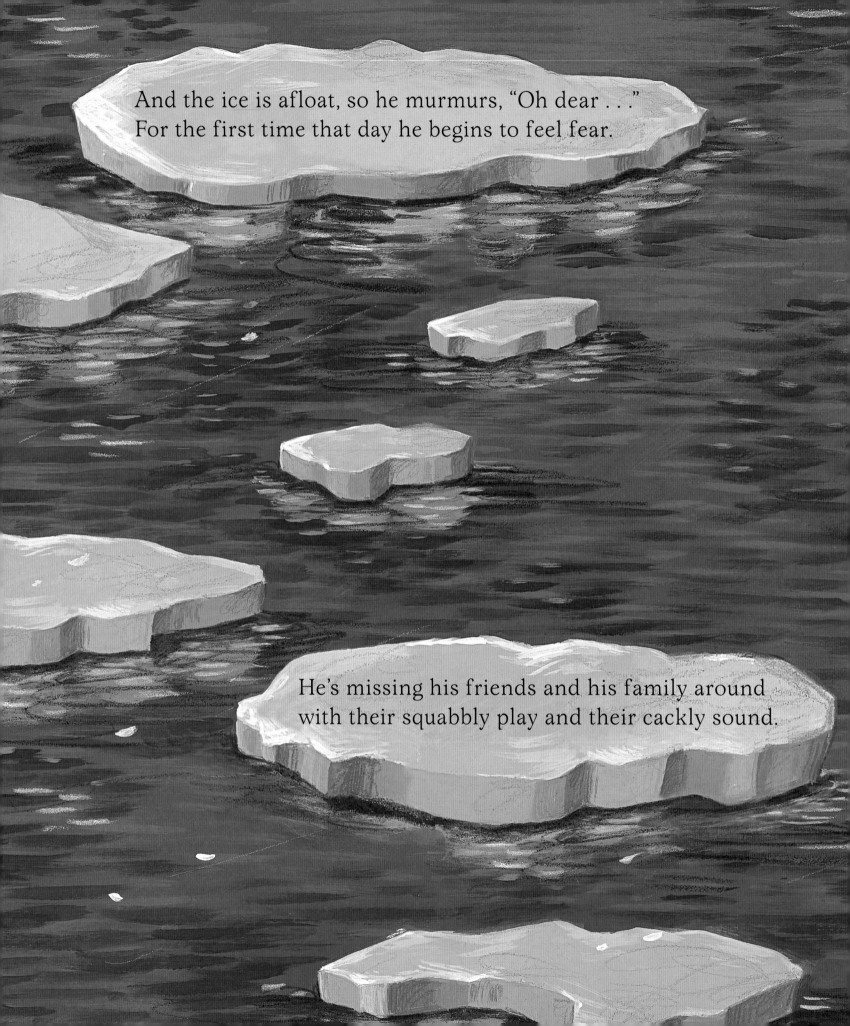

And the ice is afloat, so he murmurs, "Oh dear . . ."
For the first time that day he begins to feel fear.

He's missing his friends and his family around
with their squabbly play and their cackly sound.

How will he find them? What will he do?
For now the sea's looking more black than it's blue . . .

But what's this? The ice floe has stopped with a bump –
it seems to have met with a knobbly lump.

It's come back to land – what wonderful luck!
Penguin jumps off with a small, happy cluck.

He can see some dark shapes and he hears a soft croon.
And there by the light of the Antarctic moon . . .

. . . he makes out his mother
and rushes to her
and snuggles up safe
in her feathery fur.

And the others all gather and huddle with glee
to hear all the things Penguin went off to see.

So he tells his adventures and where he has been.
And soon, when they've heard all he's done and he's seen . . .

... the penguins all cuddle up cosy and tight
and settle themselves for an Antarctic night.